Holiday Helpers

The Animals of Silver Bell Farm

Written by Michael T. Moore

Illustrated by Andrea Newland

DEDICATION

This book is dedicated to the guests of Silver Bell Farm...
especially the little, imaginative ones!

On a quaint little farm that we call Silver Bell,
Live some animal friends with a story to tell.
By day they appear to fulfill their roles,
But at night you may find they have other goals.
Let's walk through the field and head out on the trail
So that you can be a part of this charming tale.

First, you'll find our favorite family of goats.
Head down back and grab a handful of oats.
They love to be visited and can't wait to be fed.
But they may freeze up if overcome with dread.
Pygmy Fainter is the name of their breed.
Running, climbing, and jumping is all that they need.

Next to the goats are the horses of course.
They pull the wagon with plenty of force.
Listen for their hooves going clickity-clomp.
It's amazing the amount of hay they'll chomp!
You'll see them working hard like draft horses do,
Or they'll be resting, awaiting a visit from you.

Now go past the train station to the pond bank.
In the water there, you'll find our friend Hank.
He and his pals are called pumpkinseeds,
And they like to live amongst the weeds.
You may lure them closer with some food.
A worm would certainly lift their mood.

Hank has many visitors who share the pond in peace.
Some of his best buds are the Canadian geese.
They visit us seasonally on their migratory loop.
It's easy to enjoy their beauty, just beware of their poop.
There are usually only a few at the Silver Bell dock,
But sometimes it seems they invite the whole flock.

After the pond, take a ride up on the hill.
The sight of wild turkeys is sure to thrill.
Even though the flock has nothing to fear,
They'll gobble and wobble away if you get too near.
Native to the forest and steeped in holiday tradition,
Their meandering traits make unclear their true mission.

Another frequent visitor is the white-tailed deer.
They only come out when the coast is all clear.
From a distance they are truly a sight,
But sometimes they are looking to take a bite.
Don't just watch as they nibble on pumpkins and seedlings.
Scare them off and you're sure to lift Farmer Mike's feelings.

Now that you've met these friendly creatures,
Let's learn about their lesser-known features.
When the crowds leave and the farm is closed,
This is when their true nature is exposed.
Pick a spot where you won't be found,
And see what happens when no one's around.

It just so happens that the number of goats is eight.
When Santa's around, he quickly lets them out the gate.
Their horns may not be as majestic as the mighty reindeer,
But with ease they transport the elves and their gear.
They help with Santa's chores throughout the Christmas season.
They do it all for nothing, because that's a good reason.

While the goats are keeping the elves airborne,
The horses uncover their spiraling horns.
Unicorns have fun no matter what time of year,
That's why the farm's bursting with glitter and cheer.
As true party animals, they boost up the morale.
They're always a joy to have in the corral.

Things get even crazier with Hank at the pond.
It seems that someone must have waved a magic wand.
They leave the confines of their home
With a fancy contraption that allows them to roam.
The efficiency of their work is sure to astound,
Helping to care for their namesakes in the ground.

While the fish are marching in their shoes,
The neighborly geese are maintaining their ruse.
Those migratory loops are secret flight plans,
That they follow to help the overflowing mail vans.
They love to assist with every Santa letter,
Making sure that no kid gets an ugly Christmas sweater.

As the geese make their way through the moonlit blue sky,
The turkeys cook up their own special surprise.
Instead of being the main course on the plate,
They mix, chop, and dice to make food that's top rate.
Using the bounty that's found on the farm,
They take care of their friends and no one comes to harm.

There's something about the deer Farmer Mike doesn't know.
It might seem like they're destructive, but it just isn't so.
It's their artistic abilities that they like to flaunt.
They take pride in their jack-o-lanterns that they carve to haunt.
And the trimmed Christmas trees? Well as far as they go,
Every year they are known to win "Best in Show"!

It's been a long and busy night on the farm.
Now, it's time to settle down and set the alarm.
Cuddled up in one big bed, they close their eyes,
And dream peacefully until the next sunrise.
With everything we've seen, it's easy to tell,
Without our friends, it wouldn't be the same Silver Bell.

THE END

What was your favorite character from the book? Draw it on this page, take a picture, and share it with us at silverbellfarm.com.

Is there another favorite animal of yours that you might find on a farm? We'd love to see that one too!

Made in the USA
Middletown, DE
27 May 2021

40547557R00015